The Grand Charade

The Write Touch Writing Group

2018 Members' Anthology

Table of Contents

The In-Between
- Keith H. Casey -

One foot in front of the other, one foot in front of the other. I keep moving down the street following the broken white line down the center. There is no traffic, not a sign of life anywhere on this dark night. Where am I? How did I get here? Am I alone? Where is everyone? I continue placing one foot in front of the other, not knowing what else to do. The street lights are on but cast a feeble illumination. The sound of my feet upon the pavement is muffled, and all the colors are dull, not right. The curb is lined with parked cars and next to the sidewalk rise trees in front of rows of apartment buildings, not a single light on, as if no one is home, no one is there. Strange. A pall has been cast over this place, and cast over me.

I keep moving. *What was that?* Stopping to listen, I thought I heard a faint whimper. There it was again, behind me. Turning, there is a girl sitting on her knees on the sidewalk where I just looked moments before. Her head is bent down and arms at her side, weeping. At last another soul! Approaching with caution I emit a course grating sound, then clear my dry throat and try speaking again, "Are you OK miss, what is the matter?" She gave no response, no acknowledgment of me even being there. She is despondent and appears consumed by sadness. Touching her shoulder to arouse her I say, "Can I help you miss, tell me, what is wrong?" Continued sobbing is her response. Calling out in every direction, "Helloooo! Is anyone there!" I am astonished by the fact that my voice refuses to carry far and there are no echoes. I call out again and wait, my reply is only silence.

I decide to care for her and slowly help her to her feet. Gently, I brush aside her dirty blond hair to reveal a young and pretty face, make-up streaked by tears with blue unfocused and mournful eyes. She seems about twenty years old and is wearing a white blouse and black dress slacks. Most of her weeping has now ceased except for an occasional tremor of a sob. Placing my arm around her shoulders I guide her onwards. It's time we found someone to help us, it's time to get some answers.

After traveling several deserted blocks we stop under a street light to rest. I release the girl and she sinks down to her knees just as when I found her. Caressing her hair to try and comfort her I say, "We should rest for a minute, don't worry, we will find someone to help," glancing around dubiously I add, " somewhere." Thinking out loud I say: "Why is there no-one here? Where has everyone gone?"

"The real question is: where are you?" Boomed a voice from the darkness. Startled, I turned just in time to see a form emerge from the shadows. Into the light came a tall handsome woman with long dark brunette hair draped over a curvaceous frame. She strode to us projecting confidence and strength, stunningly beautiful.

"Who are you?" I said.

"My name is Rosealee Thompson, and who are you?"

"I'm, I'm...I can't remember!" I said in sudden realization.

"Don't worry, it will all come back to you, if you are here long enough."

"Here long enough?" I questioned, "Where exactly is here?"

Ms. Thompson moved in closer, "Haven't you found this place a bit unusual? Look around." She gestured, "It's always dark, the light doesn't carry far, sounds are muffled, colors are almost all washed out of everything." She smiled as she circled us, "There is no wind, no birds, no bugs, only a rare visit by souls that never stay long, like you."

"If you know where we are then tell me, where are we?" I demanded.

"We," she stated firmly, "are in *The In-Between.*" And with that she folded her arms, grinning.

"The In-Between!" I repeated sarcastically, "In between what?"

Her grin turned into a beaming smile. Leaning closer she said in whisper: "In between Life and Death."

"That's crazy!" I spouted.

"Crazy?" She shot back, "You don't even know who you are yet! I remember who I am, others that I've talked to eventually remember who they are and even how they got here. There are only two ways to go from here and one is to go back to our lives among the living and the other is to fall into death itself. Mostly people here just die, but some find a way back among the living, where they chalk it up as a near-death experience. We," she indicated the three of us, "are stuck for a while, in between." She must have seen a puzzled look on my face and the doubt in my eye. "Look," she continued, "I met this elderly gentleman a while back. He told me that he had come across a teen-aged boy on the beach." She motioned to the distance, "Over that way about twelve miles, anyway as they talked they happened upon the boy's body, in a strangely lit up area of the beach, as if the place was basking in sunshine in only one spot. The boy bent down and touched his own body, suddenly he could see lifeguards doing CPR on him. The boy began to cough and then there was a blinding flash of light. The man found himself alone again and the bright spot on the beach faded to dark, like the rest of this place."

"That is a fantastic tale." I added.

"And that's not all." Her tone now took on an iron-like seriousness. "A few days later, while he and I were exploring this place, the old man grabbed his chest and fell." She paused, as if caught up in what she was about to say. "He reached out to me but before I could take his hand he turned into a black form. It wasn't *just* black, it was like a void, complete emptiness, absolute nothing." Rosealee was obviously still deeply affected by this. "He was gone," she murmured, bowing her head and hiding her face with her hands. When I went to comfort her she sprang up

4

and stepped away. Starring off into the distance she affirmed, "Like I said, only two ways out of here."

While trying to absorb all that she had said, something popped into my mind and I announced: "My name is Nathan! Nathan is my name."

"Your memories will all return slowly," she maintained in her deep feminine voice, "if you are here long enough. So who is this with you?" said Rosealee as she squatted down to examine the girl.

"I don't know; she doesn't speak. I'm trying to help her."

"She's a suicide!" blurted Rose, holding up the girl's arms in the dim light. You could see deep gashes across both wrists but no blood.

"I must save her," I implored, "*We* have to save her!" The look in Rosealee's eyes possessed a hint of dark foreboding.

"OK then," Rose relented, "We have to find her body, and get her back to it. Time flows differently here, much slower, so there still may be a chance to save her. Where did you find her?"

"Back that way a few blocks." I pointed, worried now more than ever. So we both gathered her up and began to retrace my steps. Being as gentile as possible we moved as quickly as we could. The girl was becoming more distant and less responsive. Many minutes passed before it became obvious the girl needed a rest. While we all sat on the curb I broke the silence, "Thank you for helping."

Rose stretched a wry smile across her pretty face, wiped her hair from her deep dark eyes saying, "It's the least I can do, you know I don't get much company here." So we shared a laugh as we caught our breath. Then, helping the girl to her feet once again, we continued.

After traveling a block more I began to wonder about rose, "Rose, you seem to know how someone might get back to the real world, why haven't you tried?"

She stopped, released the girl to me and faced me with both hands on her hips, "I'm never going back, *NEVER!*" She shouted.

"But why?"

"That's none of your damn business!" she snapped, gruffly grabbing the girl's arm and pulling her down the street.

Why would she be so defiant and sensitive about going back?, I thought.

"There!" A determined Rose said pointing. A few houses down there were lights streaming from second story apartment windows. I recognized the spot on the sidewalk where I had first found the girl.

"Let's help her up there." said Rose, but as we moved her towards the stairs the girl became combative and fought us off, terror fiercely emanating from her eyes. Breaking free, she ran to the exact spot where I had found her and began whimpering again.

"Come on," I hollered as I climbed a few stairs, "she should be fine there, lets go up and find out what's going on." The door was unlocked so we let ourselves into the kitchen. We found the girl's body lying on the floor with both wrists slashed and two small pools of blood. A bloody razor lay nearby. I sank to my knees at her side.

"Nathan, I don't know if we can help her." said Rose solemnly. She held up an empty pill bottle, and indicated several other empty pill bottles on the table.

"We have to try!" I said. "We'll get her and carry her up here if we have to!" We bolted back down the stairs but before we could reach her she slumped over and began to turn black.

The darkness pulsated as it slowly covered every inch of her form. Then it darkened further into an absolute black, not just black but an abyss, an emptiness you could feel in the pit of your stomach, a stark absence of anything, an absence of everything. Then it all seemed to blur, getting fuzzy on the edges as the pulsating returned, smaller and smaller the darkness shrank until inevitably, only a vacant sidewalk remained. The vision of what I had just witnessed and the predicament that I now found myself in came crashing home. It frightened me and shook me to my core. Looking at Rose a few feet away she had her fist to her mouth, eyes wide in horror and the color drained from her face. I went and wrapped her protectively in my arms, for her sake as well as my own. She trembled as we held each other, her stern demeanor gone, replaced by softness, by need, by the comfort we afforded each other. After a few minutes I could sense her composure returning, muscles tensing, posture straightening, so I released her and stepped back. The apartment lights faded and went dark.

"If you don't want that happening to you then we had better get moving." She choked, not yet fully recovered.

"From that direction", I pointed, "I don't remember how long I walked or where I could have started from." Rose nodded and together we left that place.

As we went, I began to wonder about Rose, who was she? "Rose, tell me a little about yourself. I barely know anything."

Forcing a smile, she put an arm around me as we walked, as good friends who have shared a hardship might. "I started modeling in high school and by the time I left college I had fashion design ideas of my own. I grew tired of my boss *borrowing* my ideas while hitting on me so I sidestepped into a new firm, one that gave me a chance to design as well as model. I made a successful place for myself there and I sure do miss it. Now, how about you Nathan?"

"Well I-I" , I stammered and then shrugged my shoulders, for those memories had not yet returned. We both began chuckling and then laughed, a great release from the horror we had both witnessed. In a few moments we spotted light in the distance and began to hurry.

The roadway came to a tee in front of a hospital emergency room. All the lights were on beaming against the gloom. "This is it, It has to be it!" Rose said in excitement as she bounded for the doors. Just then something caught my eye and I paused, above on the third floor was a room with lights shining brightly. "Come on, come on!" she urged while holding wide the door. Once inside we began searching, no one in the waiting room, no one at the desk, no one in the exam rooms.

We stood there stumped until I said, "Wait, there's one more room tucked in the corner over here!" We both slid open the curtains and there I was, lying on the bed. My shirt was off and my body was battered and beaten, blood trickled out off the corner of my mouth and my nose. Bruises and brush burns were everywhere.

"Now," instructed Rose, "The old man said that the kid laid down into his body, merging with it. The kid then cried out to him that he could now see rescuers giving him CPR before he vanished entirely in a blinding flash of light. Let's go!" She helped me up. I blended right into my body, my legs and lower torso merged but I sat up stalling for a second.

"Rose I, will I ever see you again?"

She hugged me then kissed me long and deep. "No", she whispered, and pushed me all the way down.

I awoke in my hospital bed hooked up to IVs and monitors. Seems I had been riding my motorcycle when some old man changed lanes and ran me off the road at 45 miles per hour. Good thing for me that someone had seen it and came to my aid. What a remarkable dream I had while I was unconscious for two days. I guess a Double-Major Concussion can do that to someone, well, me specifically this time. Although they almost lost me, the doctors said my recovery was progressing nicely and after 3 more days released me from the hospital. A nurse wheeled me down to my waiting cab. Opening the back door a thought hit me like being struck by lightning.

I sent the cab away and walked around the hospital to just outside the Emergency room. I looked up at the 3rd floor windows I had seen all lit-up in the supposed *In-Between*. Securing a visitors pass I soon stepped off the elevator, and found the room with its door slightly open. I went in.

A heavily bandaged figure lay in the bed as monitors beeped and clicked. Both legs were missing below the knees and the left arm ended before the elbow. Bandages covering the face barely obscured the horror beneath.

"Do you know her?" said a nurse suddenly behind me, startling me out of my trance. "She's Jane Doe number 4 this year."

I ignored the question, "What happened?"

"She's in a coma, must be 5 or 6 weeks now. She was found besides the tracks, must have been hit by a train while out walking. All they could find on her was this picture in her jogging clothes." The nurse opened the bedside drawer and handed me a card out of it. It showed a woman proudly holding up a dress for all to see.

Bleary-eyed I turned to the nurse and said, "Rose, her name is Rose, Rosealee Thompson." Then I stepped forward and held Rose's hand warmly in mine.

"The In-Between"
A Dreamstory by Keith H. Casey
Digital Art by KHC
Sketch by Beth Fifield-Crane
Copyright (c) 2019, All Rights Reserved

Be Careful What You Wish For
- Keith H. Casey -

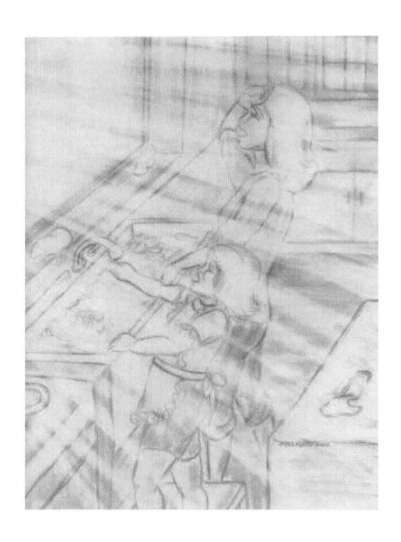

The morning sun filtered in through the kitchen window as a little girl helped her mom dry the breakfast dishes. In the background a TV was droning on, bringing with it all the terrible news from around the world: war, famine, and brutality.

The little girl spoke up, "Mommy, I wish the world could live in peace." Mom glanced over to her young daughter and smiled. Just then it got very bright outside. Light blazed into the room with extreme intensity, bringing with it heat. Too much heat.

The solar flare was unusually large. Our sun had not had such a gigantic flare in many eons. The shaded side of the planet Mercury melted. Venus shed its acidic atmosphere. Underground ice on Mars became flowing water once again.

The Earth? Life goes on. Microscopic organisms buried deeply into solid rock thrived far below the burnt out surface of the world. Planet Earth lived in peace again.

The little girl's wish had come true.

The Surprise Feast of Dr. Fu Man Chu
- Keith H. Casey -

Doctor Fu Man Chu was leaving his favorite nightclub when he noticed a rather plump cat slip into an adjacent alley-way. Smiling broadly, he quickly followed.

Images of luscious meals at his brother's Chinese restaurant danced dizzily through his mind as he licked his lips with a ravenous anticipation. Dr. Chu had brought many stray cats and dogs on a one-way trip through the backdoor, then eagerly awaited his scrumptious reward at one of the tables inside.

Nervously glancing around in the dark, he sighed in relief at a glimpse of movement, the feline was at the back of the dead-end alley. Slowly the doctor approached, rubbing his hands together in glee and salivating at this, his latest catch.

Speaking soft, gentile words, he reached down to retrieve the cat. With a hissing snarl the cat slashed out. Startled, Dr. Chu withdrew his wounded finger to his mouth which became tainted with the taste of blood. Strangely, the cat moved towards him growling deeply, haunches and back raised, tail inflated boldly. This was getting tiresome and definitely not worth the effort, but as he turned to leave several threatening growls emanated from the shadows.

Slowly emerging into the dim light came three scruffy and rough looking dogs accompanied by, of all things, several scrappy cats. Now it was he, Dr. Fu Man Chu, who was cornered.

14

Suddenly from behind, the first cat struck, leaping onto his head and savagely burying its claws deep into his face.
Bellowing, Dr. Chu grasped the cat and pulled, its claws tore out of his flesh as he flung it to the ground. He stumbled and fell, clasping his wounds as pain seared him, but there was no escape as they were all now upon him… and Dr. Fu, became chew, man.

The Surprise Feast Of Dr. Fu Man Chu

Copyright © 2007
All Rights Reserved

The Grandest Charade of Them All
- Thomas Childs -

1966-- not a particularly noteworthy year historically, but it is significant for me personally, because in the autumn of 1966, I started kindergarten. I don't have many memories before that time, but I can account for my whereabouts ever since, thus 1966 is about where my direct memories of human history begin. Half a century later, in the autumn of 2016, I reflected upon some things that transpired during my lifetime thus far.

Humans have made real progress in some areas. DNA technology, computerized fingerprint identification, and video surveillance have made us much better at catching and prosecuting the appropriate criminals. Black people gained civil rights, respect and equality, at least by law (though certain white folks still could use some opinion changing); in 1966, blacks still endured much segregation and degradation. Cigarette smoking is now prohibited in almost all indoor public places; in 1966 there were almost no public places (including workplaces) where cigarette smoking was prohibited. Lead was in all automotive gasoline in 1966; today no lead is in gasoline. The internet came along, which made communication and information storage fast and easy, though this might be a mixed blessing. What concerns me is what hasn't changed during my lifetime.

Human progress seemed to have stalled in the area of energy. Energy is important because it is needed for all human activity to exist. In 1966, cars and trucks ran on gasoline and diesel. In 2016, cars and trucks ran on gasoline and diesel, with just a small amount of alcohol (maybe 6%-- based on energy content). So where is the progress? Where are the mass produced electric cars? Where are the hydrogen cars? Whatever happened to the promise of a society powered by pollution-free renewable energy?

True, there has been *some* progress. Solar panels were invented and mass produced. Skyscrapers became more energy efficient. Cars became more efficient. But some changes might not be significant; they may be cosmetic or propaganda or just done to shut environmentalists up for awhile. Sun and wind make up only a small percentage of our energy production. And if during a given time period, cars became 10% more efficient, but 20% more cars got added to the road, was this really "progress" or just mitigation of a step backward? (And remember that nearly all vehicles still run on *fossil* oil.) And how about that commercial, where smiling people promise that 30% of our electricity will be made by clean renewable sources by 2030. Only 30%? I'm not smiling.

There is so much that could be done but so far hasn't. We illuminate billions of lights at night all night every night in buildings that are closed for business after hours and unoccupied by humans. As long as we're still generating much of our electricity by methods that deplete and pollute (coal and gas), maybe we should shut the lights off when nobody's there. (Turn them on only when intruders are present.) Very few rooftops of houses have solar panels and/or solar hot water heaters. What if every unobstructed south facing rooftop in America were covered with solar panels and hot water heaters? And then there's transportation. On a regular basis, cars get stuck in traffic jams in cities, where they idle their engines, wasting precious oil while belching out huge amounts of carbon dioxide into the atmosphere. What if we developed an efficient system of public transportation for both people and cargo in the cities and parallel to interstate highways? What if driverless taxis ran on railroad or magnetic tracks and were controlled by a master computer, timing them so that they would move through intersections at high speeds without ever stopping or colliding? Fossil fuel promoters say total clean renewable energy is too difficult, and that we should bet all our chips on fossil fuel, but is this reasonable, considering that the long term chance of human success by fossil fuel is 0%? (I'd pick difficult over impossible any day.) Yes, total clean renewable energy will be difficult, but have we ever really tried?

Oil companies try--- but in the wrong direction. The U.S.A. once had an extensive system of electric trolley cars. The oil companies destroyed these solvent businesses willfully, by buying the companies that ran them, burning the trolley cars, and ripping out the tracks and selling them for scrap metal (to ensure the trains couldn't ride again). Why? So they could replace them with diesel busses and get us to burn more diesel and burn it faster (making more money for the oil companies). What a kind considerate thing to do to future generations, who might also like the diesel, but won't have any because that past generation burned it up as fast as they could. And oil companies successfully fought hard to keep toxic lead in gasoline, decades longer than it needed to be, as less toxic alternatives to tetraethyl lead had been invented. Why? The oil companies held the patent to tetraethyl lead, but did not have patents to alternatives. Anything for a buck. I hope there's a hell for the souls of these people to happily reside.

Presidents try too, sometimes in opposing directions. Jimmy Carter placed solar hot water heaters on the roof of the White House, to symbolize America's commitment to clean renewable energy. Within two weeks of taking office, Ronald Reagan had the fully functional panels torn down, presumably to demonstrate his hatred of both Democrats and environmentalists. (One of these panels is now in a museum in China.) Why heat water with the sun, which is free, never runs out and doesn't pollute, when one can heat water with fossil fuel, which costs money, depletes a non-renewable resource and does pollute? You might think that Americans would have learned something since the days of Reagan, but no. Nearly four decades later, in 2017, Donald Trump proudly withdrew U.S. participation from the U.N. Climate Change Conference in Paris, a meeting of nations dedicated to the lowering of carbon dioxide pollution in the atmosphere. Trump thus ushered in a new U.S. "golden age" of a pollute-all-you-want policy. (The U.S. now joins Nicaragua and Syria as nations that don't participate in the CO_2 control summit.) What a bold and courageous thing to do in 2017--- take a stand for more pollution instead of less. Congressmen applauded Trump after he announced this withdrawal. As I watched this speech, my heart just sank. Never in 52 years have I been more ashamed to be an American. I am also ashamed to be a human being right now and to some extent even ashamed to be alive. Maybe we should be like China, where in some places people walk around with masks, and even according to the Chinese government, countless die due to breathing emissions from coal burning power plants.

Ah yes, those emissions. Each year, humans dump 38 billion tons of carbon dioxide (2.4 million pounds per second) into the Earth's atmosphere, all released from burning coal, oil and natural gas. Mainstream science tells us that this extra CO_2 is causing the Earth to warm, and this might wreak havoc on sea levels, coastal populations, weather and ecosystems. Some people however feel that this global warming effect is not even real, or at most overrated; that the Earth's warming might be part of a natural not-yet-understood cycle (not caused by burning fossil fuel). Some feel that if the Earth does warm, this effect will be slight and not so bad after all. I'm not sure what to believe, but I suspect that climate change deniers support their views mainly by money-driven-science (backed by coal, oil and natural gas) rather than fact-driven-science. Beware of money-driven-science. Remember that money-driven-science once "proved" that cigarette smoking was completely harmless. Also, while it is plausible that the effects from CO_2 added to Earth's atmosphere will prove to be less harmful than mainstream science suggests, it is also plausible that the effects will prove to be far more harmful. (Remember that mainstream science once believed that chlorofluorocarbons were relatively harmless gasses. They are now known to be detrimental to Earth's ozone layer. Mainstream science also once believed that DDT wasn't harmful--- they got that wrong too.) My position is that I would rather error on the side of safety, and unlike Trump, I believe that it is not alright to use Earth's atmosphere as an industrial toilet of convenience, to appease man's never ending appetite for waste and poor decision making, or because we are just too damn lazy to come up with solutions.

In much of the world, there has been a growing movement to transition from dirty finite fossil energy to clean renewable energy. However, progress has been too little, too slow and too late. To say that now is the time to start abandoning fossil fuel is the understatement of a lifetime--- 1966, the year I started kindergarten, should have been about the time humans began this project. Had this been done, I could have grown up in a country that I would have been proud of.

Instead, I must live in this real world. If I were to die soon, and had the opportunity to leave a detailed message with my grave marker, to be read by someone centuries from now, I would describe this last half a century as a time of lies, broken promises, and multiple missed opportunities, all driven by greed, indifference and stupidity. I would describe a time when almost nothing of significance took place. I would describe our nation as a place where (based on population percentage) people got more and more college degrees, yet collectively still managed to remain idiots.

Still, there may be reason to hope. Countries other than the U.S.A., such as Iceland, Sweden, France, are taking clean renewable energy seriously. Even some tiny island nations, with about the population of North Tonawanda, have already converted to 100% electricity made by wind, sun and water. France now makes 90% of their electricity from non-carbon sources. And some countries even have the phase out of fossil fuel written into their constitutions. Tell me-- What would happen if in the U.S.A. we tried as hard to implement clean renewable energy as the fossil fuel industry tries to defeat it? We spend a lot of time and effort making excuses as to why clean renewable energy is impossible. What if we instead spent that time actually making clean renewable energy happen? I think we would have been well past the half way mark by now.

All this brings me to the topic of the day: *charades*. Of all the charades ever perpetrated by man, in all of history, human prosperity, based on fossil fuel, is the grandest of them all. It is also the worst idea humans ever came up with--- worse than the holocaust and even worse than the nuclear arms race. If we don't transition to 100% clean renewable energy, and do so in a timely manner, then we are not a thriving species, we are a dying species.

There is another and somewhat lesser charade that many of us humans partake in: the belief that we are powerless to change the world for the better. I don't know whether or not there is a God, but either way, humans don't seem to be bound into predetermined outcomes. We have free will. We could choose to be nice to each other, instead of worshiping the money god and selling out our fellow man for a buck every chance we get. We could choose an energy path that would allow life for mankind as a whole, instead of a path guaranteeing the deaths of most people and the demise of the most technological societies. And we could do this even in this backward, third-world country known as the U.S.A.

The Big Blow
- Beth E. Fifield-Crane -

In the beautiful coastal town of "Nice View", life is peaceful and easy. Neighbors all get along and there is no crime. In fact, the only spirited discourse you will hear is when you stop into "The Old Tavern" at night.

Every night Jim Pratt and Rick Wills show up at the tavern at seven o'clock on the dot to hold court. Now Rick and Jim have been friends all of their lives, but they are both the kind of guy who is always right, and they always have to one-up each other. This can lead to some lively and fantastic discussions.

One night after a few beers, Jim asks the young barman Tom, "Do you remember the big blow of 79?"

"No sir," Tom replied, "I wasn't born yet."

Jim says, "Well, pour me another and I'll tell you all about it."

As Tom turns to get Jim's drink, he rolls his eyes at the bar back, nodding his head toward Rick knowing what was coming. Jim starts,"'bout four o'clock that afternoon the ocean starts to churn. As the sky turned dark as night the wind came blowin' in. The waves start to rise and fall higher and higher. I says to the captain, 'We're in for a big blow. I'm goin' to get my family and batten down the house.'"

"I was strugglin' against the wind on the upper road, cause I knew the lower road along the beach would soon be covered in water. I was 'bout a hundred yards from the rise in the lower road when the first wave came in floodin' everything but the tree on the rise. All of a sudden I hears a tiny voice,

'Help me! Please, help me!' "When I looks over the cliff there in that tree is a little girl. So I reaches in my bag for the fishin' net I was takin' home to mend. I ties one end of the net on an outcroppin' of rocks and throws the net toward the tree. Not wantin' the girl to panic, I starts talkin' to her as I'm climbin' down.

"What are ya doin' in that tree, little one?"

"She reaches in her jacket and pulls out a tiny kitten and says, 'My kitten got stuck in the tree so I came up to get her, then the water came and we can't get down.'"

"'Well, tuck her back in safe,' I says."

"As she did, I snatches her up and tells her to hold on tight and climbs back up the net. Then I took her home to her grateful parents and went on my way."

"HA! HA! HA!" booms out from down the bar. It's Rick.

He said, "That must'a been the busiest tree in the world just after four o'clock that day. When Josh Bert got there as the first wave hit, he pulled a man from that tree. Then when Sam Watson got there as the first wave hit, he pulled a teenager from that tree. Next comes George Wilson and he gets an eight-year-old boy from that tree as the first wave hits. Now you save a little girl with a kitten no less!!! HA! HA! HA!"

Rick turns to Tom, "Pour me another and I'll tell you a true story how I saved a woman and her three kids from the roof of their cottage on the beach."

Winter (Haiku)
- Beth E. Fifield-Crane –

Summer like the leaf

Is falling ever gently

Into winter snow

The Forbidden Forest
- Beth E. Fifield-Crane -

In the forbidden forest there are inhabitants galore.
From the tips of the treetops to beneath the forest floor.

The fairy queen that ruled the forest was the best in the land.
When there was a problem she'd send a helping hand.

Her handmaidens bandaged bunnies and a bird or two.
She'd send them to the sick to feed them healing dew.

When her subjects were hungry she said, "Open the palace
        stores."
If the weather was frigid she said, "Open the palace doors".

The queen knew, well-fed and warm, everyone would behave.
So the only danger in the forest was the evil spider's cave.

There were signs in the forest to stay away from the cave.
For if the spider caught you, you'd be his food or his slave.

There was a tiny young fairy whose name was Lil.
Everyone in the kingdom said she had a strong will.

Lil would run, jump and tumble all over the place.
She approached everything in life as if it were a race.

She'd wrestle bugs and climb up the tallest trees.
And she always had scrapes on her elbows and knees.

Playing near the spider cave Lil saw a handmaiden go in.
She thought, "I'll follow her although it's a sin."

She crept up to the cave and silently opened the door.
Peeking in, what she saw made her faint to the floor.

When she woke a giant spider cradled her in one arm.
The spider said, "Don't be afraid, Lil, I'll do you no harm."

Lil said to the spider, "That's the queen's crown on your head!
Did you make her a slave or worse is our queen dead?"

Shaking her head "No" while stroking Lil's hand.
She said, "Let me tell you a story of a witch from our land."

"A witch who lived here grew up to be cruel.
So she had to be banished during my mother's rule."

"As the witch left the court she cast a spell on me.
'A giant spider forever you will be.'"

"My mother hid me here, afraid that I'd be killed.
Because when it comes to spiders, people are strong-willed."

"Because spiders are ugly, everyone thinks we are mean.
So I live hidden here, but, Lil, I am your queen."

The Eye of Mother Nature
- Steven A. Greene -

The eye of Mother Nature opens to reveal her inner light, which guides us on our earthly journey. The sunlight cascades downward to warm our spirit, helping us to endure our time in this world.

Soon we all leave to tend gardens in different realms, cultivating that which cannot be sown or grown in this life.

Only our physical form perishes, our spirit lives on with all our relations that have gone before, waiting patiently for those who'll follow.

Do not be sad, for they have arrived home and await you and I.

Love's Mirage
- Steven A. Greene -

She walks across the windswept sand
Painted Raven soars above the land
Her path meandering mindlessly
Both spirits knowing "what will be, will be"

Little lizards dart and run
The Sidewinder, seeks refuge from the sun
Two bodies traveling different paths
Two Spirits, trying to find their way back

They've been separated for so long
The sand dunes sing their spirit song
Will it be their destiny or their fate?
Will they finally find their long lost mate?

The desert is anything but cool
It can be hot and oh so cruel
She looks up to find Painted Raven
All she sees is the glare of the sun

She listens intently for his cry
She sees an image in the corner of her eye
Is that the beat of his wings on the wind?
No, just the sound of her heart trying to mend

He searches the dunes while he is flying
Gasping for breath, feels like he's dying
Love is hardly ever what we're told
Only the blessed together, grow old

Death Valley, or the Valley of Death
Is this where they finally meet?
Or take their last breath?
Hot and dry or cold and cruel
This is where Mother Nature rules

If allowed to meet face to face
It is only by "Creator's Grace"
Will they leave, venerated?
Or must they always be separated?

Dreams or Real
- Steven A. Greene -

I'm stuck in that space between my thoughts. I can see everything that's happening, but it seems like I'm just a bystander in my own life.

It is sort of like a dream, everything is in color and motion. Sometimes flying by, other times, it's in slow motion. I am very indecisive and don't have control over my thoughts or actions.

I am able to split into multiple beings and multi-task like never before. It's just that at times it doesn't seem like I'm accomplishing anything at all. I can carry on a conversation within my being and it is normal. Nothing strange at all about this, or so it seems to me. I look about to see if anyone else is watching and realize that I'm the only one here.

There are different shadows being cast, but by who? I notice the movement out of the corner of my eye but when I concentrate and stare directly at them they disappear. Are they really there or am I imagining them?

Am I asleep and dreaming or am I awake and imagining everything. I have no idea. Could this be because of lack of sleep, since I'm working 12 hours, 5 pm to 5 am? I find it very hard to get more than 3.5-5 hrs of sleep on this shift.

Oh, I hear the dogs fussing and the phone is ringing. Have to go out and let them out of their kennel for awhile, then tee time at eleven. I can't wait for retirement.

Real or Surreal
- Steven A. Green -

When I finally met it face to face, panic hit me like a cold bucket of water. I didn't know if it was fear or the cold rivulets of water running down my spine, that was making me shiver, like a dog shitting razor blades.

I couldn't help staring into those mere slits that were its evil yellow eyes. They penetrated to the inner most core of my being. I was frozen in place, that pathetic limbo, as my body was unable to respond to my brain's instinctual survival commands. "Run away, as far and as fast as you can."

Is this how the prey feels as it stares into the viper's eyes, just before the deadly strike? My brain racing a million miles per hour and my body frozen in time. I could not stop the tears from running down my cheeks and almost lost control of my bladder.

Everything around me disappeared except those evil eyes. It was as if those yellow slits and my watering eyes were all that existed anymore. A standoff that it was clearly winning.

Panic, there was no other word for it.

Just when I felt it could not get any worse, a snout with a forked tongue flicking in and out of it, began to form in front of my eyes. Was it my imagination, or was that face beginning to smile in conquering satisfaction?

I felt a stirring around my ankles that began to rise up my calves and thighs. It felt like coils being wrapped around me, then tightening as they progressed up my body.

Out of nowhere a mirror appeared and exposed my body exuding blood from multiple slashes on my body. It was surreal in a horrible way, because I could see the coils of the viper tightening around my body, squeezing out my life's blood, but I could not feel it.

It became real as the intense pain radiated to my brain. Every command for my body to move was trying to travel the neuron highway in my body, to no avail. I was about to scream out, when the coils suddenly wrapped around my chest and neck. Those screams of pain and panic died in my mind, unable to find their way into the world.

As I felt life's breath being extinguished from my pathetic body, I decided to try escape, one last time. I would not quit.

As I struggled, with everything I could muster, I awoke to find myself wrapped tightly in my sheets, hanging halfway off my bed.

Was this just a dream, or was it an omen of things to come.

SHE
- Steven A. Greene -

He saw her as she entered through the double glass doors. Deep down in his soul he knew his world would never be the same.

His pulse raced, his blood heated and his heart seemed like it was ready to burst forth from his chest. Instant infatuation grabbed a hold of him as he caught sight of her curvaceous body stretching the fabric of her short dress to its limit. Her ample breasts accentuated the V-neckline of her dress.

As his eyes feasted upon her beauty, her luscious lips parted in a slight smile, which he perceived as one of recognition. He did not know this woman except in his dreams.

Her raven hair, falling past her shoulders bounced as she approached him. Her olive complexion did not possess any trace of imperfection. Her teeth sparkled like shiny pearls in the moonlight. Her well- toned legs extended well past the hem of her short crimson dress and ended in feet encased in matching red stilettos. There was a diamond bracelet around her left ankle that matched her earrings and the ring on her right hand.

She had covered the 20 feet separating them in 10 paces as she seemed to flow towards him. As she approached, he was transfixed on her steel blue eyes that didn't seem to blink.

He never suspected, let alone saw the 10 mm barrel, as the hollow-point projectile entered his forehead directly between his eyes and exited with the back of his head in a muffled thud.

He would never hurt another human being ever again. He had not seen her in a dream, she was his last nightmare.

Society of Human Elimination

40

T 4 2
- Helene Rose Lee -

Esme and Hank had reached an impasse of sorts in their marriage. Now that the nest was empty of their three children, they had time for each other, something they had looked forward to for twenty-eight years.

As an added bonus, both took early retirement from their teaching jobs to fulfill their plans to kick back, travel and simply ignore the alarm clock in the morning. They even sold their family home and bought a condo to cut down on the hours spent maintaining a house. One of their favorite times of day was "Tea Time" at four every afternoon.

About five months into this arrangement, Hank noticed that Esme became irritated with the smallest infraction of her neat house look. A brown leaf on a house plant had her running for the small pruning shears. And Esme noticed that Hank was really a slob, leaving his clothes, his clubs here and there. And when she tripped on the golf club bag, a contained explosion spewed forth between gritted teeth.

Small battles became big battles. One of his jobs was to change light bulbs when they blew. But did he? Sort of, after twenty or so reminders. And when Esme decided to serve fried chicken for dinner one day, Hank blew up. How could she forget that his stomach could not tolerate fried food.

Finally, both decided to separate, perhaps divorce. So Hank took off with his clothes and clubs to rent a small apartment, while Esme settled into a single life that suited her just fine. But, she missed Hank and truth be told he missed her.

After several weeks of not speaking, he called and asked her to dinner at a very nice restaurant. This was the beginning of their "dating" period until one day when Hank called to say that he had a surprise for Esme and she was to open her front door and look to her right.

Naturally Esme did so and there in front of the next door condo stood Hank holding a *For Sale* sign. With a dramatic gesture he threw it on the ground and said, "Hi neighbor."

So now both were happy, resuming the tea for two ritual, occasionally going to the movies together, to lunches, shopping, even those long awaited vacations or intimate bliss. But at other times, if they so chose, each retired to his or her own abode to live their own life styles, while respecting the other's life. And both feel they each have the perfect mate and the perfect neighbor.

The Stranger In My Kitchen
(Or Murphy's Law)
- Adrienne Mecklenburg -

It had been a long, hard day at work. Murphy's Law, anything that can go wrong, will, was in full force.

First, I was late for work because of the trains. One had broken down, affecting everything behind it. Then I spilt my coffee on my skirt when I tried to catch the Egg-McMuffin I had dropped. There went breakfast. I had to buy a new skirt making me even later. In the office, both the copier and fax machines broke down. From there it was all downhill.

I was going through a nasty divorce and to end my day on a real low note, my husband called jut to harass me about the temporary upkeep the judge ordered him to pay. Why he complained I couldn't understand. The amount was only $500 a month and it wouldn't even pay my rent. He was quite wealthy and for him it was small change.

Reaching home about six thirty that night, I was exhausted and couldn't wait to make myself a cup of tea. Hanging up my coat and kicking off my shoed, I headed for my kitchen. I was rather startled to see a naked stranger standing at the stove with his back to me. He was tall and from what I could see of him, he had a body to die for. Prophetic thought.

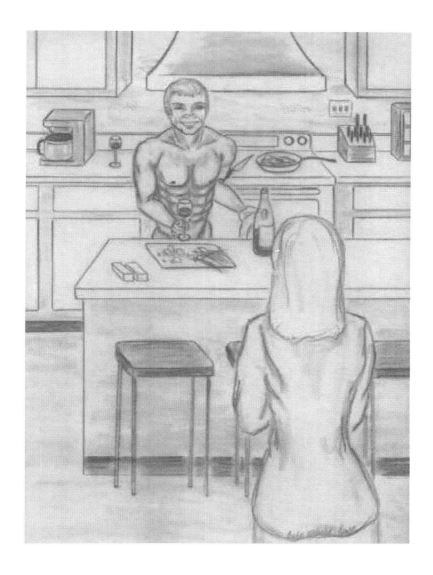

I yelled at him demanding to know who he was and what he was doing in my kitchen at my stove. He calmly turned around and with a smile, offered me a glass of wine.

'Oh my,' I thought. He had it all. Then I looked into his eyes and a chill of fear went down my spine. They were dead eyes, like a shark's or a leopard's eyes.

Trying to keep my cool and hoping to distract him, I asked what he was cooking.

"Steak with sautéed onions, baked potato and a small salad."

"That sounds absolutely delicious. I like my steak rare, please," I said.

"This is just for me after I finish my job," came his cold answer.

"What job is that?" I asked, already knowing the answer.

"Killing you," he laughed, a frightening, insane laugh.

All of a sudden, he grabbed my large carving knife from the stove where he had laid it. As he came at me, the only thing I could grab was the two sticks of soft butter on the counter. Murphy's law again. He laughed as he continued coming around the counter at me and I threw the softened butter on the floor in front of him. Being so soft, they splattered. Still laughing, he took another step toward me and stepped on the butter and slipped. Grabbing the edge of the counter, he tried to stop himself but fell awkwardly to the floor. He landed on the knife and it went right into his heart, killing him instantly.

Murphy's Law at it best.

I called 911. When the police got there and heard my explanation of what happened, they said I was lucky. The body was removed and taken to the morgue for an autopsy and identification. The man, Michael Smith, was ruthless, vicious murderer for hire and was wanted in connection with about ten other deaths. After along investigation, they told me it was my husband who had hired Smith to murder me.

My now ex-husband should be happy, he doesn't have to pay me alimony. Since I was still married to him at the time of the attempted murder, I got it all: the house, car, yacht, the money and the condo he had bought just before the attempted murder.

He was found guilty of conspiracy to commit murder and doesn't have to worry about where he'll live for the rest of his life. He has a twelve by sixteen foot room he shares with a roommate. A very large, tattooed roommate.

This Woman of Mystery
- Adrienne Mecklenburg -

Twenty years ago, Winston Shepard murdered his young, beautiful wife, Jewel, and the banker he thought she was having an affair with and got away with it. Until now.

As he lay in his bed, he remembers that day and the look of fear on her face as she fought for her life. He strangled her then took her body to the rocky ledge and threw her body into the water far below. He convinced everyone that she had run away with Jason Holt a prominent banker in town who had mysteriously disappeared the same day and was never seen again.

He smiles, remembering the way her tongue stuck out and how the light of life left her eyes. Gleefully, he remembers the way Holt begged for his life as he slowly buried him alive, after he shot Holt in the knees and elbows. For several years, he was the prime suspect in the disappearance of his wife, but without a body, the police could never prove anything,

She walked out of the fog, heading for the gray stone house, this woman of mystery. Looking up at the house, ugly in the daylight, but now steeped in the velvet darkness, she saw a light go on in that room and shuddered in fear. Continuing up the grassy pathway to the door, she was about to knock. A hawk's feather floated down, softly landing at her feet and a chill ran through her body. She turns to run back but stops and turns around. Steeling herself, she rings the doorbell and hears it echo through the house. No one answers, so she knocks. The door, unlocked, opens and she goes in.

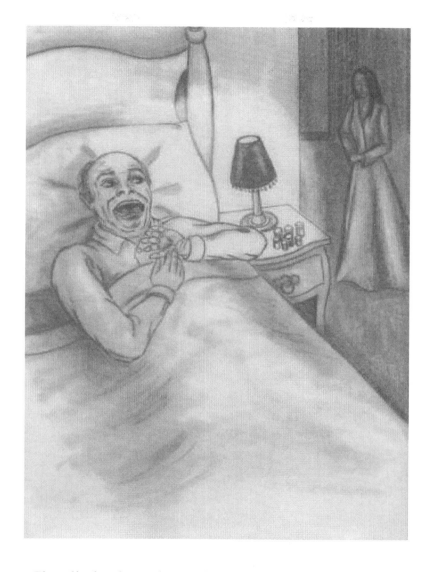

She climbs the stairs to the top floor and going down the hall, she enters THAT room and stares at the man lying in the bed, dying. He sees her and screams in terror. He cannot see her face but knows who she is and screams at her to go away. Is she the ghost of the wife he brutally murdered so long ago in the bed he was now dying in.

"I've come to say good-bye to you," she softly says.

She turns and walks from the room, smiling as she listens to his screams of terror,

His doctor and Minister were coming to tell him that they had a new heart and he was to go to the hospital for a transplant when they heard his screams. They ran into the house and up to his room.

The woman, hearing them come in, stepped into a darkened alcove.

When they reached his room, he told them his dead wife ghost had come to haunt him, they thought he was becoming delirious as death approached. Then they heard the soft footsteps going down the stairs and out the door. Running down stairs and out the door after her, they only saw a woman in a white dress with long black hair disappear into the mist. They didn't know if she was a ghost, spirit or real.

This woman of mystery.

They tried to convince him he had imaged it. Winston won't listen to them, he just kept saying he had killed them both and to call the police. He was so agitated, the doctor, after administering a sedative, called the police. Before he died, he confessed to the murder of his wife and the banker, telling them everything.

Wearing a long black vail, the woman of mystery attended her husband's funeral. No one knew who she was. Six months later, Jewel, with her lawyer, came back to town to claim her rightful inheritance. She told them that when she went over the cliff the tide was higher than usual because of a storm out at sea.

"I got extremely lucky and was swept away from the cliff wall and a fishing boat pulled me from the water. I had no memory of who I was or what happened to me. They took me with them, and the Captain, who was quite old, took me to his home where his wife cared for me as though I was their daughter. After many years my memory finally returned, and I remembered the horror of that night. Before Winston strangled me, he made me watch as he shot poor Jason then buried him alive. I'll never forget Jason's screams as the dirt slowly covered him. He couldn't even push the dirt away because both his elbows were shattered. All I want is what's rightfully mine. I will make sure Mrs. Holt gets a share of Winston's estate."

Three months later, after proving who she was, Jewel was declared the sole inheritor of Winston Shepard's vast estate. She sold the mansion, giving the proceeds from the sale to Mrs. Holt as she promised. After disposing of all of Winston's personal belongings, she disappeared one day into the mist.

This woman of Mystery.

Who Killed the Handsome Male Model
- Adrienne Mecklenburg -

Tom was a tall, good looking, well built male model. He had just stepped out of his shower when he heard his phone ringing. Hoping it was a new gig, he wrapped a towel around his waist and hurriedly went to answer it. The phone was on the table in the living room and just as he reached it, it stopped ringing.

Disappointed, he turned to go back to his bedroom to get dressed when he realized his apartment door was open. A chill of fear ran up his spine and the hairs on the nape of his neck stood up as he went to close it. Turning back, he stopped cold. There was a stranger standing in the bedroom doorway.

He was supposed to have dinner with his beautiful fiancée, Madeline, also a model, at one of the most elite restaurants in the city. When he didn't show up, she went to his apartment and found his bloody, mutilated body.

The police were called to investigate. They questioned his fiancée, a rival model who wanted the same job, and Madeline's crazy ex-boyfriend and several other tenants in the building. The police were suspicious of Madeline and her supposed ex-boyfriend, but they had good alibis. The police investigated the homicide for nearly two weeks but found nothing.

The question of who killed Tom and why, would remain unsolved for several years until the day the D.A.'s office received a confession from the hired killer detailing how he got into the apartment and who hired him.

Was it his fiancée, when she found out he was going to end their engagement? Or maybe it was the jealous rival, or perhaps Madeline's ex-boyfriend? Or was it all three?

He Walked With A Limp
- Mike Miller -

We grew up together, same grade school, same high school. I called him Izzy. Maybe it was Dizzy. He answered to either. I don't know his real name.

Lost touch with him after graduating. I went on to college for a year, I heard he went into the Army.

He came home at Christmas one year, looking great in his uniform, so many friends high-fiving him, partying with him. I was invited by his friends. He waved to me, we shook hands "how's it goin'?"

He was to get engaged, I had never seen the girl before, English was her second language, a distant second language. Anyway, attractive, quite attractive.

By New Years, he was on his way back to his assignment, his girl stayed with his sister.

I didn't hear much about him or his girl for months.

On the radio, breaking news: Isaac Roblee was injured in an IED (improvised explosive device) attack while he was patrolling in a Humvee. Not life threatening. More information to follow.

I didn't make any name connection.

The next morning, an update: he suffered serious injury to his left leg in the ambush, and was being transferred to the Army Hospital Germany for treatment.

Several months later I was invited to a welcome home celebration for Izzy. It seemed like he was coming back too early from his tour of duty. I went to the event; there he was, ribboned uniform, wheelchair, holding a baby, his girl pushing the chair.

A couple of months after the welcome home a politician sponsored a basket raffle fund-raising event including donations from family, friends, businesses, and other politicians. Izzy, the girl, and the baby were there. A contractor donated modifications to their home, a ramp, a walk-in shower, an exercise room. A car dealer donated a specially equipped van.

And someone gave him a job.

He disappeared from the news for a couple of years.

* * *

The news reported an armed robbery attempt at a convenience store at closing time on a Saturday night. The register and the safe were emptied.

I was the last customer at the store that day, potato chips and Pepsi, talking with the clerk. The robber wore a mask, long sleeved shirt, long pants, gloves, and track shoes. I wrestled the gun away from him, but he ran off, far out distancing me. I thought I recognized his voice. It sounded like Izzy. Maybe Izzy had a brother.

The investigator took the robber's gun and asked me many questions: whether I might know the robber, how I was able to wrestle the gun away from him, do I remember any identifying marks or mannerisms, on and on. For what seemed like hours. I answered as best I could. I mentioned Izzy because of his voice, but I told the investigator of Izzy's disability; I knew it wasn't him.

I was invited to view a lineup. Izzy was in the lineup. Five men walked onto the stage, Izzy limped on. I didn't recognize anyone other than Izzy, and after it was over, I saw Izzy hobbling with a cane away from the station, accompanied by his girl, and three little ones. Why the police thought Izzy was involved puzzled me.

It became a cold case, unsolved for six years. I saw Izzy from time to time, the same girl, the youngsters growing, and each time, a new one in tow. He was always hobbling around, using a cane and sometimes driving his specially equipped van.

One day, I saw him, I thought. He didn't recognize me. Playing pick-up ball. At first I didn't give it a second thought. Either Izzy has a twin, or there's someone who looks like him, or his recovery was a miracle.

I figured I might surprise him by yelling out his name. "IZZY!"

But no response. I wanted to try his last name but I didn't remember it.

Suspecting that he might recognize my voice, I asked a friend to call out his name. "IZZY!" No response.

I ran over to the court, but whoever it was, had already walked to his car and was driving away.

I asked some classmates, few remembered Izzy, fewer remembered Izzy's war injury. I looked up newspaper articles over the years since his injury and I located the house that was specially converted for him. Lights were on; door was open. The yard had not been mowed in months, the porch railing, what was left of it, was hanging on only by rusty nails.

I mustered the courage to knock on the door. A young boy came to the door, a couple of kids playing in the background, and a toddler. I asked if his father or mother were home. "Mom, someone's at the door."

"Hello. You don't remember me, but I was a classmate of Izzy back in school. The last time I saw him was at the welcome home party for him years ago or maybe it was the fund raiser. We weren't close friends, but I've often wondered about him."

"He's not here."

'When will he be back?"

"He's not here."

"Is he okay?"

"Who sent you?"

"No one, I just wanted to find out about him."

"He disappeared, someone said PTSD."

"Did he go for treatment?"

"For a while."

"Do the doctors know where he might be?"

"They won't tell me nothin'."

"Where was he treated?"

"It was downtown, near the park, near the mall, that's all I know. They asked me to go with him to the center a couple of times, but he always said no."

"Does he have family? Can they tell you anything?"

"His sister doesn't call or even return my calls. She stopped about a year ago."

"Any other family?"

"His parents, but I saw them only once, at the fundraiser. They never spoke to me."

"How are you holding up with your family?"

"Not good. I get some money from someone, I don't know who, deposited in my account on the first of every month. It helps. My family sends money too. I get food stamps. The neighbors sometimes help out."

"How many kids do you have? Five, 1, 4, 6, 7, and 10."

"What's your name?"

"Maisey. That's what they named me when I moved here."

"Do you mind if I go to the treatment center and try to find out what happened?"

"They don't tell me anything. They won't tell you anything. Who cares anyway?"

I decide to take a chance on learning about Izzy at the center. I was never in the service, but I find an Army cap for $1 at Goodwill. With two days stubble growth, grubby clothes and gardening shoes I drive downtown, find a parking space some distance from the center, and walk to it. People stare.

I walk up the ramp and hit the automatic door button. The receptionist, the sign says AMY, a young girl finishes something on the computer, then looks at me.

"Yeah."

"I knew Izzy from the Army, and I hear he is living here."

She answers the ringing phone; I hear half a fruitless conversation."

"Who are you looking for?"

"Izzy. I knew him form the army," pointing at my cap.

"Are you family?"

"Not close, sort of cousins. I know his wife and their kids. I visited them a couple of days ago. She told me he is here."

"Let me page the administrator."

I busy myself looking through some magazines. Phone rings.

"Someone here from the Army, asking about Izzy. He knows the family, says he's a cousin. What do I tell him?"

A faint conversation.

"Is that all I can say?"

A faint conversation.

"Can I tell him about Dr Karen."

A faint conversation.

I spot a rack of business cards, and take a card for Dr. Karen, crumble it and place it in my pocket.

Amy whispers "Oh, oops, sorry, I didn't know."

A faint conversation and Amy hangs up the phone.

I look away from the magazines. Amy says, "Izzy isn't here anymore."

"When did he leave? Do you know where he went?"

"A few weeks ago."

"I heard his Doctor's name was … wait a minute, his wife gave me the doctor's card, I have it here somewhere."

I fumble around in my pockets, crumble the card one more time and pull it out.

"Here it is, Dr Karen."

"I don't know if I should tell you this, but Dr. Karen resigned from the center the day after Izzy was discharged."

"Can I talk to her?"

"We don't know where she went."

"Is there someone else I could talk to here?"

"No."

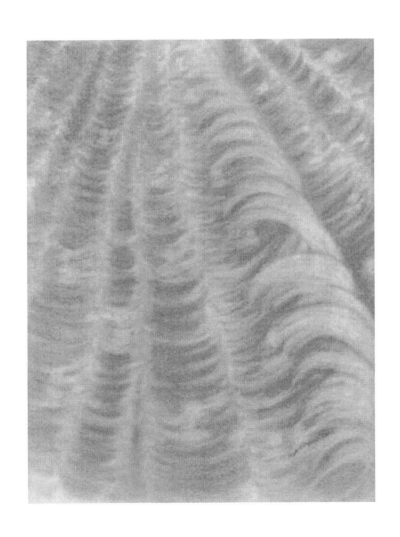

Waves
- Mike Miller -

A boat cruising
In a creek
Leaving waves behind
The boat may be long past
But the waves continue
In its wake.

So too in life
A parent, a sibling,
A wife, a child,
And others.
Creating waves while
Passing through.

We may not
Have seen the boat
But we see
The many waves
The wake.

And in death we see
The many waves
At the wake.

The Case of the Dubious Witness
- Annette Szymula -

The 911 call came in at 0300 hours. The voice on the phone sounded like a young boy of perhaps eleven or twelve, his voice breaking occasionally as he described a frightening domestic incident.

"Some guy bashed in the front door and started fighting with Nickie and choking her. I had to save her, so I stabbed him with steak knife, and he ran out. Then I grabbed Nickie's phone and hid in the pantry," he explained in hushed tones.

The operator's stomach tightened as she tried to calm him and keep him on the line, while she activated the dispatch radio to alert officers in the vicinity. She told the lad to stay in the pantry and wait for the police to arrive. Within minutes, she heard the din of doors bursting open and officers yelling in the background, and she breathed a sigh of relief.

"The cops are here!" yelled the boy. "Thank you, Ma'am. Now, I gotta go!" The line went dead.

The police officers found evidence of a struggle, a bloody steak knife on the counter, a bloody hand print on the pantry door, which was closed tight, and a trail of blood droplets leading to the back door. They carefully pulled the pantry door open, and they found a young woman, crouching behind the door. Her eyes grew wide. She held up blood-stained hands and squeaked in a shrill, breathy voice, "What happened?"

Both officers quickly holstered their weapons, and the female deputy spoke in a soothing voice, "Miss, you are safe now. My name is Nora Tracy, and this is Luis Perez. Please do not touch anything, until we can swab your hands for evidence, and ask you a few questions."

Perez ran back to the squad car and returned with a satchel. He pulled some equipment out. He swabbed her hands with Q-tips, dropped each into a separate vial and placed each into evidence bags. Then he carefully scraped under her fingernails and did likewise. As he proceeded, he explained that since this was a small town, officers on the night shift had to gather preliminary evidence. The county forensics team would arrive in the morning for a more thorough investigation of the crime scene. He proceeded to collect samples of the blood by the back door, and he dropped a blood tinged cell phone from the floor of the pantry into another evidence bag.

As he finished his work, he looked around and asked, "Where's the boy? The one who called 911."

The woman looked baffled and shook her head, "What boy? I live here alone."

Tracy frowned, pulled out her notebook, and said, "Well, Miss, why don't you tell us your name and what you know about what happened tonight?"

"I'm Veronica Truax. I guess I must have gone to bed last night about ten. I woke up just now in the pantry. I don't know how I got here. Honest!" the young lady answered, tears brimming in her eyes. Then she noticed the tight fitting mini dress she was wearing, and muttered, "Where's my nightgown?"

Tracy and Perez exchanged glances. This was going to be a long night.

They persuaded the victim to let them drive her to the hospital, so that her injuries could be documented. When Tracy had accompanied the young woman to her bedroom to retrieve another set of clothes, she noticed that the closet contained mostly conservative tops, pants and sensible shoes; no sexy party dresses. Yet, a fishnet stocking dangled from the lid of an old trunk in the corner. After they arrived at the hospital, Veronica had a panic attack and fainted during the examination. The doctor cracked an ammonia capsule, which made her patient wake with a start, obviously trying to get her bearings.

"Am I in a hospital? Thank, God! I thought I was a goner!" she exclaimed in warm alto voice. Then she gave Perez and Tracy a quizzical look and added, "You're cops, right? Did you catch that monster?"

Tracy raised her eyebrows, fumbled for her notepad, and blurted, "But you said you couldn't remember the attack. If you do now, we need a description."

A worried look flashed across the woman's face. She brought her hand to her mouth, chewed on her index finger, and muttered to herself, "Not again."

Then she straightened, looked Tracy square in the face, and declared, "I'll never forget his face. I can't believe someone so handsome and nice could turn on me like that. If you have a pen and paper, I'll draw him for you. After the doctor finished her exam, she took Tracy's notebook and pen, and sketched a face. Meanwhile, Perez keyed notes into his tablet as Miss Truax described the events of that night. Her boyfriend had called to admit he had met someone else. Their quarrel upset her, and she couldn't sleep, so she decided to change her clothes and walk to a neighborhood bar. She danced with a tall, blonde, blue eyed hunk, and let him walk her home; then he forced his way into her place and choked her when she resisted his advances.

"I started to black out. I thought I was going to die. Then I woke up here," she said and gave Perez a lopsided smile as she handed Tracy her notebook. "Good enough? I love to sketch; I minored in art."

The portrait was quite detailed, better than most courtroom illustrators' drawings that Tracy had seen. She gave her a thumb's up, and handed it to Perez, who nodded approvingly. The sketch would save hours of paging through mug shots. The officers let Veronica clean up and change in the ladies' room, bagged her minidress, and drove to headquarters. Tracy was intrigued by how friendly, confident and helpful Veronica seemed now. Perez smiled. It was 0600 hours; with a little luck, they could deliver the evidence, get the woman's signature on a complaint form, then file their reports before their shift ended at 0800 hours.

At the station, the team separated. Perez headed to the squad room to log the attacker's portrait into the system and to issue an all-points bulletin about the suspect. He placed the evidence bags into a secure locker in the forensics lab and strode down the hall whistling, pleased at how quickly he and his partner seemed to be on track to solve this case. He met Tracy at the coffee machine and they headed towards the interrogation room, where Tracy had left Veronica dozing with her head on the table. As they entered the room, Veronica woke with the old panicked look in her eyes. Once again, she claimed she could remember nothing and that she just wanted to go home.

Perez plunked his cup down, leaned over the table, and yelled at his witness, "What the heck is the matter with you? An hour ago, you drew us a picture and gave us a blow by blow account of the attack. Now you can't remember? This isn't a game, young lady! There's a dangerous man out there, and we need your help to catch him! Stop this nonsense!"

Tracy placed a hand on her partner's arm, gave him a warning look, and took over the interrogation. She had an unsettling feeling as she observed the woman's expression morph into a menacing glare. Veronica threw her arm over the back of the chair, cocked her head and glowered at Perez. In a low, menacing voice she growled, "You're mean. Don't bother Veronica! Veronica is really scared, and she can't think when that happens!"

Startled by the sudden transformation, Perez raised his hands and backed away. Tracy's mind reeled as she recalled her psychology lectures at the academy. She explained in a gentler tone, "He's just frustrated, because we'll need you to file a formal complaint to press charges. Otherwise, when we catch the culprit, we'll have to release him. You don't want that, do you?"

"No. I'll sign whatever I have to. I'll do it for you," the young woman answered gruffly, giving Perez a withering look. "I don't like him. You better keep him away from Veronica."

Tracy quickly agreed and sent her partner to print out the complaint form. She offered the victim some coffee, but she asked for soda pop. Tracy walked her to the vending machines. She noticed how different her gait and demeanor seemed now. It reminded her of her own kid brother's loping shuffle. Very strange. This was one interview for the books.

When Perez returned with the complaint form, Veronica perused it intently.

"What's an assail-ant?" she sounded out; then nodded as Tracy explained the term. She signed the form with a strangely child-like script as "Ronnie Truax".

Perez looked at the woman with alarm, and asked, "Is that your nickname? Could you please use the name on your driver's license?" He didn't want to screw up. The prosecutor would never forgive him, and his captain would never forget it.

The woman looked at her signature and frowned. She seemed to be debating with herself, as she mumbled, "Uh-oh, I can't fix this. I better split. You gotta do it. You gotta be strong, Nickie." Then, she looked back at Perez and told him to be nice to Veronica. The young lady began to shift in her seat. Her head drooped. She heaved a huge sigh, shivered, sat up straighter, and crossed her legs.

She looked down at the paper, bit her lip and gave the officers a baleful look. With a trembling hand, she grabbed the pen and whimpered, "I am so sorry. I don't mean to be such a nuisance. I just…When bad things happen to me, I-I get these episodes. I-I get confused. Ummm…Where do I sign?"

Tracy pointed to the signature line. She watched as the woman wrote "Veronica" in front of "Ronnie" and placed parentheses around the nickname. Or was it a real name? A sinking feeling hit her stomach, as she realized she would have to get a psych exam on a potential witness, who just might be profoundly disturbed. She offered to drive the woman home when her shift ended, much to her partner's relief.

On the way home, Tracy gently probed again, "Just between you and me, who are Ronnie and Nickie, anyway? They aren't just nicknames, are they?" She had to know.

Veronica sighed, "Ronnie was my brother. He used to tease me by calling me 'Ickie, Nickie, Veronickie'. When we were kids, there was a bad flood, and he helped me climb into a tree to avoid the rushing water, but he lost his grip and drowned. The last thing he said to me was to not worry; he would always come back to help me." Her lips trembled, and she continued, "Ever since then, sometimes when I am in a frightening or really stressful situation, I get these blackouts. I don't always remember what I do when I'm like that." She shook her head and wiped away tears, "I guess, I'm crazy."

Tracy patted her shoulder. "No. You're not. But I know a psychiatrist who might help you cope better, maybe remember better. If you testify in court, it would help if you see him first, so the defense can't mess with your head too much."

Veronica grimaced and nodded, "Oh dear. I didn't think of that. I haven't seen a shrink in years; I thought I was okay now, but after tonight, I-I don't know." She sighed, gave Tracy a rueful smile, and continued, "I'll make an appointment. I have to learn how to control myself; or should I say, myselves?"

"Just remember that you are a survivor. You are stronger than you think," Tracy reassured her witness, but the officer worried about how the girl's condition could impact the case.

Tracy dropped the young woman at her home, and she cautioned her to stay out of her kitchen until after the forensic team came later that day. She glanced at her watch. It was 0930 hours. It had been a long night. Once they caught the perpetrator, it was going to be really challenging to help the prosecution with such a dubious witness. She prayed that the real Veronica would show up at the trial.

ESPERANZA
- Annette Szymula -

The name on the gate read Esperanza, which means hope, but an aura of disenchantment permeated the place. Autumn had lost her luster. Crinkled, brown leaves skittered across the road. A steep, deeply rutted gravel driveway led up to our destination. The antebellum mansion had dominated the hill overlooking Lake Keuka in the Finger Lakes for nearly two centuries, but it had clearly seen better days. Clapboards were missing, several windows were boarded up, and the massive columns supporting the portico were weathered gray.

According to local legend, the original owner had built a veritable fortress in the wilderness in order to allay the fears of his city bred wife. The Greek revival mansion had walls that were twelve inches thick and shutters both inside and out. The current owners were in the process of restoring the dilapidated property and turning it into a trendy art gallery. Scaffolding creaked in the brisk wind, while piles of lumber and heavy equipment littered the front lawn.

To help with expenses, the owners had agreed to rent the old manse to a cinematography student, who was intent on producing a film to complete his graduate degree. With the help of his faculty advisor, Ron had assembled a motley crew of film and theater students from various local colleges to work for him *gratis* for the experience of being in a real, albeit amateur, movie.

Thus, I found myself alighting from his professor's station wagon, with a couple other student actors and the make-up girl.

After several weekends spent filming at outdoor locations during particularly blustery Fall weather, it was a relief to have a roof over our heads. Cast and crew huddled around a space heater and the one working fireplace. The only other amenity was a large coffee urn that dispensed a bitter, black brew whose one redeeming quality was that it kept our fingers warm in the otherwise unheated upper floors of the building.

There was always an undercurrent of excitement at the beginning of each shoot. The chatter of conversations among former strangers produced a background buzz, while Ron prepared to film. College students bemoaning dull lectures and project deadlines, amateur theater actors brooding about their characters' motivations, the drama professor fretting about rewriting a scene due to the absence of a key actor that day, added to the cacophony of the crew members shouting about angles and F-Stops, while they tried not to trip over a snake pit of tangled electric cords. For better or worse, each of us had committed our time and talents to help Ron fulfill his dream. By now, the cast members knew the drill. Our job was to paint our faces, don our costumes, stay out of the film crew's way and wait to be called for our scenes. At first, it was fascinating to watch the guys set up each scene, but it often took over an hour for them to get the lighting and camera angles just right. Fighting the inevitable boredom and the chilly drafts, I forced down a cup of steaming, black coffee and followed the signs to the restrooms.

Downstairs, I was pleasantly surprised to find modern fixtures. However, once I closed the door, I realized that an eerie silence had enveloped the room. It was so quiet, I could hear my heartbeat. The very walls seemed to press in on me, as if to whisper their secrets. My hands trembled as I reached for the faucet, and I felt genuine relief to listen to the sound of water splashing in the sink. Grabbing a towel, I quickly dried my hands and rushed out the door.

Hurrying down the empty hallway, a sense of foreboding overwhelmed me. I pushed back one of the shutters and peered out the grimy, wavy pane of antique glass. The hills and fields surrounding the oddly shaped Finger Lake looked tranquil now, but I wondered how isolated the lady of the house had felt in her new home. How did she cope when left alone, waiting for her husband to return from his business trips to far off Albany and Buffalo? Did the deep valley caress and comfort her, or did it feel claustrophobic? Did she bloom where she was planted or wither away into madness?

In the distance, someone called my name. I shivered and drew in a deep breath to calm myself. I had never believed in ghosts, but I had the unnerving feeling that the mansion was trying to speak to me. I bounded up the winding staircase two steps at a time, trying to block the images that wracked my mind, and sought the familiar clatter of the camera crew.

It felt good to step under the hot lights and act my part. Suddenly, it was easy to pretend to be the perplexed innocent ingénue, while pseudo-hippies milled around in their post-Woodstock frenzy until we all heard the magic words, "Cut. That's a wrap."

Over the next few weekends, my curiosity gave me the courage to explore the rest of the mansion when I was not needed in front of the camera. I chatted with the caretaker and won his trust. One day, he told me he had noticed something "real cool" upstairs, while clearing out antique furniture. Together, we climbed the stairs to the attic. There was one huge oval window illuminating the space, and a finger of light brightened a patch of color under one of the gables. It revealed a fresco of a young woman reaching out to two children, who were rolling hoops on a lawn, seemingly oblivious to her presence. I stood there, silent as the rafters, enthralled by the painting.

"Who painted it?" I whispered. The caretaker startled me with his answer.

"I don't know, but you are the spitting image of her. Kind of spooky, isn't it? I'll have to show Ron. He'll probably want to shoot this painting, too. You wait here. I'll get him."

He slammed the door, and his clunky footsteps could be heard retreating on his way down the stairs. Left alone, I peered around the attic space, cluttered with the detritus of generations of occupants, who had lived and died within these walls. In the gable opposite the fresco, a rusty bed frame stood next to an antique washstand topped with a beautiful pitcher nesting in a matching bowl, chipped from daily use, and covered with dust and cobwebs.

A cool draft wafted over me. I felt a cold knot in my stomach as my gaze returned to the painting. My fingers rose up, against my will, gently touching the woman's hands. The walls throbbed with memories. A young mother smiling, bouncing her babies on her knees, singing lullabies as she tucked them into bed. An anxious wife gazing out the long windows in the hallways below, hoping for her husband's safe return. A gracious hostess entertaining guests, resigning herself to more days trapped in her elegant prison, while her husband's success in business and politics kept him away. A panicked woman gazing at her blood-stained handkerchief, despairing of a cure, realizing she would not live to see her children grow up. A stoic artist, quarantining herself in the attic while she painted an icon to protect her precious children, her legacy.

My reverie was barely broken by the excited chatter of Ron and his crew as they hurriedly set up their equipment before the light faded. I heard his directions as if through a glass wall.

Like a puppet, I let Ron pose me in profile with the lady in the painting. I was acutely aware of our similarities: our hair the same long, golden blonde; our fingers so delicate and thin, her gown my favorite shade of blue, her wistful smile reflecting mine. My eyes surveyed the rest of the attic, dim except for the camera lights and the dusty streams of sunlight from the oval window. Something compelled me to walk towards that window. Halfway there, I looked down and noticed that the light and shadows had encased my feet in a web-like pattern.

In a dull voice, I called to Ron, "Looked, I'm trapped."

"Neat! Let's try some *cinema verité*," he gushed, as he removed his camera from its tripod and circled me to film my silhouette against the window. Then he tracked my movements as I crumpled to the floor and hugged my knees in a fetal position.

I ad-libbed, "I can't stay here. If I do, I'll be doomed like the woman in the painting. I have to go!"

When I ran for the door, Ron followed me, camera a-whirling, as I raced down three flights of stairs. I didn't stop when he yelled, "Cut".

I scurried out the front door and onto the lawn, bending over, inhaling deep breaths of air to clear my lungs, my head and my heart.

It was a relief to finish filming at Esperanza. I could never shake the depressing visions of a life half-lived. When Ron finally held an informal premier for his film in a small theater at his college, the cinematography and editing were quite impressive. The attic scenes exposed my uncanny resemblance to the woman in the painting. They have haunted me ever since.

Years later, I drove by the old mansion, which had evolved into a winery and had been restored to its former glory. Alas, the heavy iron gates were locked. I fingered the cold metal bars and whispered a prayer for the lady in the painting, thanking her for inspiring me to live my own life to the fullest, knowing that the spirit who once roamed the halls of Esperanza was a benevolent, maternal one. I hoped she was finally at peace.

St. Valentine's Day
- An Essay
- Susan M. Wright -

It's Valentine's day and I decided to do a little research from my personal library.

I started off with one of my favorites. The Dictionary of Mythology, Folklore, and Symbols by Gertrude Jobes. Although it was published in 1961 not much has changed.

Valentine, 1) Masculine name from the Latin meaning healthy and powerful 2) See Saints.

A sweet heart chosen on St Valentine's Day in accordance with the belief that birds begin to mate on February 14th.

Next entry: *St Valentine, Martyred Feb 14, 269. Imprisoned for assisting persecuted Christians and he restored the sight of his jailers daughter. Then he was beat to death. Portrayed as a young priest bearing a sword. Other attributes, bow and arrow, Cupid, Heart, Heart pierced by arrow. Knots of red and blue ribbons, roses and spring flowers.*

Cupid - Roman god of first-born love. He's a complex little fellow, but I'll make a long story short. He represents the overcoming of a spirit by love. He is a warrior and a conqueror. His golden arrows represent virtuous love. His name is from the Latin cupido, meaning desire, passion.

Great place to start, on to the World Book encyclopedia. According to them there were two St. Valentines, The first was beheaded by Emperor Claudius II for marrying young men. The Emperor believed that single men made better warriors so no marriage. St. Valentine performed secret marriages, got caught and lost his head. The second was a great story teller loved by all children. He refused to worship the Roman gods and landed in prison for his faith. As the story goes the children missed him so much they slid notes through the bars of his prison cell window. Is this where the Valentine tradition started?

Some scholars think they may be the same guy, and there was no mention of healing in the World Book, who knows. News turns into stories and stories into legends. It wasn't till 496 that St. Pope Gelasius I declared February 14th St. Valentine's Day so... who really knows.

There are all sorts of theories floating around about how the whole mixture of sword yielding priests and birds choosing mates while fat little cupids flit about piercing hearts with love's sharp arrows became the whoop-la it is today.

Some are of the opinion that it all started with the ancient Romans. Every Feb the 15th the festival of Lupercalia took place. As protection against wolves young men went about hitting people with thick strips of animal hide. The crazy thing is women jumped to take the blows because everyone knows a good whipping makes a woman more fertile. Yikes!

The so-called experts are quick to add that the date is so close and love and fertility are included in both. In the year 43 when the Romans started their takeover of the British Isles they took over the customs and beliefs of the locals by keeping the dates and changing a few names here and there. You can absorb and reshape a nation in a few generations with good story telling.

Here's a fun fact I knew, but forgot. It was said that birds chose their mates on February 14. In 1561 the powers that be or, should I say, were, changed the calendar, jumped back 10 days and added an extra day every 4 years, This got the calendar of man back in tune with Mother Nature's schedule. So before 1561

Feb 14 was actually Feb 24. That means the birds had a couple of extra weeks to look for a mate. I wonder if it made a difference in their love lives.

Anyways ... During the Middle Ages the Normans spoke a language we now call Norman French. They have a word, Galantine. It means gallant or lover; Valentine, from the Latin healthy and powerful they sound a lot alike. The sword is a phallic symbol ... It's starting to add up, we have a date of origin and a basic concept of St Valentine and when he got his day.

Early references to Valentine's Day can be found in the works of poet Geoffrey Chaucer in the 1300's. A few lines from "The Parliament of Fowls"... "For this was St. Valentine's Day/ When every fowl cometh/ There to choose his mate."

He is also given credit for starting the Valentine custom. It makes sense; he heard the stories about the kids sliding notes through the prison bars. There has never been a whole lot of money in poetry so he started a new fad.

A few lines of poetry, some nice art work. Something every guy will have to get his girl if he wants to live in peace and it happens every year! Genius!!!

By the 1700's everyone everywhere had some customs attached to the day. In Denmark they still send pressed white flowers with coded messages hoping the receiver can guess who sent them. In The UK and Italy young women get up before sunrise to look out the window. They believe the first man they see will be the man they marry and if not him some one that looks like him. I'm glad that's not the custom here, I love my neighbors but .... I'd have to keep the shades down and the curtains drawn all day.

The phrase, "Wearing your heart on your sleeve" probably evolved from a custom from the same time period. Young people would write their names on heart shaped pieces of paper and put them in a hat or basket, draw names and then pin the chosen name on their sleeves. That's the sort of event where you really need to check the guest list before accepting an invitation.

During the late 1700's and early 1800's books full of verse and different ideas about making and delivering Valentine's cards were all the rage. Esther A. Howland of Worcester, Massachusetts, was one of the first US manufacturers of Valentine's Day cards. In the 1850's she was running a $100,000 per year business. Valentines cards her only product. Some were hand painted, encrusted with mother of pearl and lace and ribbons selling for as much as $10 each.

I was feeling like that was enough facts for one research session, enough to make a fun little blip with a few fun facts when my eye fell upon another of my favorite Reference Books ... the Dictionary of Cynical Quotations By Jonathan Green where I found these fun little tidbits:

"Love lasteth as long as the money endurith," William Caxton said that in 1474.

"When poverty comes in at the door, loves creeps out the window." Thomas Fuller 1732

Quoted from The Devil's Dictionary by Ambrose Bierce published in 1911:

Love, n. A temporary insanity curable by marriage or the removal of the patient from the influences under which he incurred the disease...It is sometimes fatal.

And ...

Cupid, n. The so called god of love. A Bastardly creation of a barbarous fancy.

Wow I'd love to get a copy of that book!

I will close this piece with a poem by the infamous Dorothy Parker written in 1927

By the time you swear you're his

Shivering and sighing

And he vows his passion is

Infinite, Undying

Ladies make a note of this:

One of you is lying!

The Holly-Daze and
Sell-A-Bray-Shuns
- Susan M. Wright -

I got several calendars this holiday season. The guys at the feed store and at the local hardware store both put one in my bag while I was checking out: "Here ya are, Happy Holidays!" I accepted them graciously. I like the guys, I like antique tractors and I like the guides on the back covers. There's useful advice, like, remember to change your furnace filter, it's time to plant your peas, and there are handy charts that tell how many teaspoons in a tablespoon.

My mailbox has turned into a calendar collection box, the insurance agent, the bank, and a few others from places that I do business with. Again, more helpful reminders: it's time to review your policy, make an appointment today. These I don't appreciate so much. It's expensive advertising and postage that I pay for in the long run, and it's not delivered with a smile like the others.

I resent the charity calendars that come from organizations that I've never heard of and especially the ones that come from out of state. I have compassion for Native American orphan children, I really do. However, when I get an unsolicited gift from them and a letter saying that they know I will want to give them money, well...they don't know me. "Tis better to give than receive," especially during the holidays. So thanks kids, I think

I'll use this one to mark all the things I have to do, but don't want to do, like pay my school taxes and go to the dentist.

My favorite calendar comes along with an order I had placed through the mail for some decorations. It lists all the seldom celebrated holidays, some of which I'm sure were made up by manufacturers and retailers but it is full of interesting things to celebrate that I was not aware of.

For example did you know that January 3rd is Festival of Sleep day? I'm really surprised that one hasn't caught on. January 13th is Make your Dreams Come True Day. National Dress up Your Pet Day is on the 14th. I hope no one out there has the dream of winning the National Dress up your Pet Day competition, talk about a day late. Chinese New Year and National Pie day both fall on the 23rd this year. Opposite Day is on the 25th and Backwards Day is on the 31st. To me it seems like they are the same thing, they should have held them farther apart so that you could really appreciate each individually.

February has some fun ones too. Saturday the 4th is Thank a Mailman Day. I thank the Mailman and the Mail Lady whenever I see them. They have a really hard job and the reputation for going "Postal." You never know, a little thank you every now and again might just save you some big troubles down the road. The 8th is Fly a Kite Day. I like the idea, but the timing is off. Just try finding a kite at the mall in February. The 9th is Toothache Day, what a strange thing to celebrate. Maybe dentists made this one up to make us think twice about all the Valentine's Day Candy on the 14th. The 21st is Fat Tuesday. I think that should be National Pie day too. They put it too close to New Year's Day and we all need that extra tome to break our resolutions. Ash Wednesday and be Be Humble day both fall on the 22nd. Wouldn't it be a true celebration if everyone gave up being aggressive for lent?

The holiday that I found most worthy of celebration falls on April 10th, Encourage a Young Writer Day. Wouldn't it be awesome if there was as much hype about Young Writers Day as there is about Super Bowl Sunday? Arbor Day and Tell a Story day are both on the 27th. I hope some of those young writers are there to get those stories down on paper. The 29th is Zipper Day. I'm not sure what this is all about but I hope everyone has fun?

May 6th is Nurse's Day, I think they deserve the whole month. No one gives more of them self than a good nurse. The 18th is Visit Your Relatives Day; yikes, this could lead to getting your name in the paper for all the wrong reasons. We all have our reasons for not visiting certain branches of the family tree. My personal advice on this one is to celebrate selectively and cautiously! The 23rd is Lucky Penny Day, good luck, I hope you find one. Keep your eyes open and maybe you will get really lucky and find some paper money too!

June 1st is Doughnut Day and the 2nd is National Rocky Road Day. They should have made the 3rd High Cholesterol Day! The 4th is Hug Your Cat Day. Whoever came up with this idea never met my cat. Hope the nurses at the emergency room remember me when I show up after that party.

We all celebrate the 4th of July with fireworks, but how do you celebrate Workaholics Day which falls on the 5th? The 6th is National Fried Chicken Day and the 7th is Macaroni day. Another call for a High Cholesterol Day. I never heard of Cow Appreciation Day or I Love Horses Day which both fall on the 15th. I wonder if this causes jealousy issues on the farm. I think they are both really big animals and they should both have their own day.

August 3rd is National Watermelon Day, that's a fun one. I can just see little kids smiling in the sunshine their faces dripping with pink juice, shiny black seeds stuck to the chins. The 16th is Tell a Joke Day, I celebrate this one almost every day. Mark

Twain said the laughter is the key to the universe, I think it's the music of the soul. The 27th is Global Forgiveness Day. I love the idea but don't think that humanity as a whole could pull it off.

September 12th is Chocolate Milkshake day. Now there is a holiday for the mom's out there. The kids are back in school, go get yourself a milk shake and drink the whole thing! You don't have to share today!

That brings us to Christmas. It is in the stores before Halloween and has pushed Thanksgiving out of the limelight. Thanksgiving is the holiday that is meant to bring folks together without the need for gifts, balloons, or more importantly credit cards. It's a day meant to celebrate the one thing that money can't buy, friends and family.

Christmas now fills out stores 4 months of the year when you include the ½ off sales that last until the end of January. I wonder how Mary and Joseph would feel if they could see the whoop-la we put on for their son every year. I wonder if they would notice how jolly ole St. Nick has taken over the true meaning of their son's birth? I wish National Hug Day got half as much attention. It is June 11th if you want to mark your calendar, that gives you a week to recover from hugging your cat.

I think we need to start celebrating things that don't cost money, and I don't think we have to celebrate things we are not interested in. Yes all babies are miracles, but I don't want to have to spend $50 on a Baby Shower gift because my co-workers daughter got haphazardly impregnated by some guy that's in jail now. I dread the thought of another wedding, especially when I know the marriage won't last more than a year. There goes another $100 and there's a 50/50 on whether I'll get a thank you note. Save yourself some money; don't invite me, no postage

43078891R00057

Made in the USA
Middletown, DE
20 April 2019